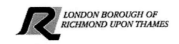
TA... L...N

ON A
SCHOOL TRIP

WRITTEN BY JULIE GASSMAN   ILLUSTRATED BY ANDY ELKERTON

You've been marking the calendar. The day's finally here!
The day you've been waiting for — the best day of the year!

It's time for the school trip, and you're ready to go.
But before you head off, there's one thing you should know . . .

School Trip
Permission

Before you leave school and head to the bus,
your teacher will have some rules to discuss.

And there will be parent helpers who won't be prepared
for a big, scaly student who might make them feel **scared**!

Once on the bus the real trouble will start.
Your dragon will kick off the trip with a **fart.**

And that great spiky tail needs its very own seat.
There just isn't room for a huge stinky beast!

When you're on a school trip, you represent your school.
Manners are important, so follow the rules.

But your dragon will flap his wings, shriek and squawk,
while the fireman is trying to give you a talk.

When it's time for a tour, things won't improve.
Your dragon will fall behind as you move.

Once back in line he'll demand you go faster.
He'll touch the wrong thing. It will be a **disaster!**

But I've told him about this school trip for weeks.
If I say he can't come, tears will roll down his cheeks.

He deserves an adventure . . . to learn something new!
Please, oh **please**, can't he go too?

AND TAKE YOUR **DRAGON** ON HIS VERY OWN TRIP!

ABOUT THE AUTHOR

The youngest in a family of nine children, Julie Gassman grew up in South Dakota, USA. After college, she swapped small-town life for the world of magazine publishing in New York City. She now lives in southern Minnesota with her husband and their three children. Julie's favourite school trip was visiting the zoo, where she spent lots of time watching the gorillas.

ABOUT THE ILLUSTRATOR

After 14 years as a graphic designer, Andy decided to go back to his illustrative roots as a children's book illustrator. Since 2002 he has produced work for picture books, educational books, advertising and toy design. Andy has worked for clients all over the world. He currently lives on the west coast of Scotland with his wife and three children.

Raintree is an imprint of Capstone Global Library Limited, a company incorporated in England and Wales having its registered office at 264 Banbury Road, Oxford, OX2 7DY – Registered company number: 6695582

www.raintree.co.uk
myorders@raintree.co.uk

ISBN 978 1 4747 8724 6

Designed by Nathan Gassman
Original illustrations © Capstone Global Library Limited 2020
Printed and bound in India